THE AMAZING ADVENTURES Of TWO BOYS

Bed Time Stories
for
Children

D. HORRIDGE

ONCE UPON A TIME CHILDREN'S BED TIME ADVENTURE SERIES

Volume One

By

Donald L. Horridge

and

D. Michael Horridge

INTRODUCTION

Once upon a time, a long time ago, these stories were told by my father to my brother and myself.

Our father's name was Don Horridge. He was a spectacular man. Each night he would come home after work, have dinner, and before we went to bed, he would tell us his stories.

His imagination seemed limitless, but as I grew older, I realized that he dipped into the deep well of his own life experiences when he was younger to develop his stories. He was born and raised in Vermont, and really did walk miles to school through the snow of winter. As a young graduate of high school, he was became an adventurer who explored the swamps of Louisiana with two other young men for nearly a year. He painted his colorful imagination from these many memories.

Our father's stories never frightened us. They were adventures of two brothers in remote lands. We were always the heroes. In the stories, our family or friends always rescued us. At "The End," we were glad to be home, but could not wait for the next sequel. He kept us spell bound as we waited for sleep to rescue us.

I'm sure his incredible imagination and storytelling kept us from going to sleep much longer than our mother wished, but his creativity ignited both my brother's and my innovations and visions. My brother is an artist and I enjoy writing. I feel privileged to append my thoughts and few literary gifts to my father's stories. I pray that this story is the first of many.

He never wrote his stories. I finally asked him to do so as he lay ill in his bed in Texas. He wrote about two thirds of this small book by hand, and shortly thereafter left for another adventure in heaven. That was in 1990. In his memory, I publish this book for all the older children who love to be read to before bedtime.

This is a story of adventure, compromise, and love. Love and respect between two brothers and parents who dearly loved and respected both of them.

I dedicate this book to my father, Donald Lloyd Horridge, a man, an incredible father, and wonderful friend. May his imagination ignite the fuse of creativity in the reader and each child who hears or reads these stories.

CONTENTS

CHAPTER 1 – ROUGH SEAS

The wind screamed through the small boat's rigging attempting to take it with it as a companion to nowhere. The black night was saturated with driving rain and the little ship struggled to preserve its dignity in the confusion of the great waves, which slammed into it. Occasionally the frog-like voice of the captain would join the bedlam, and then fade away into the roar of the storm.

In the cramped quarters below deck, the occupants of the two inadequate cabins resigned themselves to the whims of nature's anger. The boys were in one cabin and their mother and father in the other. Rich, the younger of the two slept with the peace of an angel. His natural good humor reflected itself by the smile on his face. The relaxed attitude of his slumber indicated complete ignorance of the peril surrounding the vessel. He was almost fourteen years old, with the happy, carefree ability to ignore the responsibility of trouble and worry.

Mike was sick. The nausea had been approaching for about an hour. He had never been stricken by the hopelessness of seasickness. He knew this was the cause of his discomfort and tried to ignore it by letting his mind wander amongst other thoughts. He had hated to leave the plantation but his wisdom made him realize there was nothing one could do about it.

When Dad's company had decided to make him General Manager of all the foreign investments, he had accepted, and here they were on this miserable boat headed to Talanka. This thinking did him no good. He was sick, very sick. He leapt out of bed with the only thought in his mind to reach the deck as soon as possible. The rolling cabin was not sympathetic with his emergency and immediately threw him into his younger brother's bunk.

"Yipes," screamed Rich. "What's happening?" He was in a sitting position with a startled and puzzled expression on his face that indicated some attempt to understand the cause of his sudden awakening.

"Is that you brother?" he asked.

"I'm sick Rich, I'm sick," bemoaned Mike. "I'm going up on deck."

"What's happened to this darned boat?" asked Rich. "It feels like it's ready to jump out from under us."

His question was answered with only, "I'm sick" and with the feeling that there was much going on that was currently beyond the scope of good sense he jumped up and grabbed Mike's arm. Somehow, without any sympathy from the moving cabin, they found the door and battered their way down the narrow passageway to the steep steps that led to the deck hatch. Amid Mike's pleas to hurry, they stumbled up the stairs and finally felt the stinging fury of the storm.

The only comment which erupted from the usually expressive Rich was "My gosh, what a flood!" The tilting, water soaked deck gave all indications of completely disappearing from sight at any moment. As he attempted to grab any friendly handhold, Rich's feet sped from beneath him pulling Mike to the deck with a thud. A sudden, uncompromising lurch of the deck prevented the possibility of regaining a foothold and for a moment, the brothers were suspended in a blaring, confused situation where they were at the mercy of the storm.

Suddenly, the vessel surrendered to the force of a giant wave and slammed the boys into the rail with sickening crunch.

"You all right, Rich?" asked Mike frantically, "Hold on!"

There was a muffled, "I'm okay, get off my leg," just as a wall of water angrily dumped itself onto the two struggling forms. For a second, the boat righted, allowing the boys to regain their feet, but before they had the chance to stabilize their position, a huge wave hit them and carried their protesting bodies over the rail into the raging sea.

CHAPTER 2 – OVERBOARD

For a time that seemed to stretch forever, they struggled in a wet world of confusion and chaos. By a quirk of fate, they both popped out of the water gasping for breath not more than a yard apart.

"Float, Rich," yelled Mike, "and hold onto my hand."

A victory sign with his two fingers held aloft indicated that he understood, but with a sickly nod of his head indicated that Richard had received the message but was struggling. Both boys stared into the black, angry night for the welcome sight of a friendly boat but both felt the impossibility of such a miracle. There was nothing. No lights. No silhouettes…nothing but water.

The horror of the situation seized both the boys at once. Neither one indicated his hopelessness and thoughts to the other. Mike knew the small ship was fairly close to shore, but did not know the direction of this sanctuary. He also realized that they could be gone for hours before anyone would discover their absence. If luck allowed someone to discover they were both overboard, it would be next to impossible to find them. The boat was fighting for its life and an organized search was not feasible.

Mike switched his thoughts away from these improbabilities and tried to recall the route of the ship. He had made two previous trips to Talanka with his mother and remembered that most of the time he could see the outline of the jungle shore. This knowledge was still of no value since one could only see five to ten feet into the black mouth of the storm. However, it was apparent that the storm was coming in from the sea so it would be best to continue floating on their backs and hope they would be swept to shore. Thank goodness, he and Rich were excellent swimmers and were at home in the water.

They must have floated for over two hours before the first complaints of fatigue and exposure began to be felt. The monotony of the beating rain on their faces and the rise and fall of the waves had only been broken by short comments by the boys. There were times when the storm seemed to relent but would soon dispel this false impression by renewing its merciless purpose.

"Maybe we ought to sing like those freezing people do in the movies," suggested Rich.

"Might get water in our mouths," said Mike. "Better save our strength."

"Yeah, guess so," returned Rich. "Are you scared, Mike?"

"Don't worry, everything will be all right," replied Mike. However, there was no indication of enthusiasm in his statement.

The conversation ceased amid a sudden flash of lightning and a resultant clap of thunder that rumbled its way into the lap of the storm. Rich wondered if God was mad at him. Maybe He was mad because of the bad things thing he had done. He tried to think of something that had made God so mad at him and finally gave it up since he could recall nothing that would make anyone this angry. Maybe, he thought, I should say my prayers, but he wondered just what to say. Resolving that it would be proper to request safety for all, he silently made his plea on this basis. He had just finished his amen when something brushed his leg.

Shark! The sharks had found them. A small gasp passed his lips but he immediately deadened its effect with a slight cough. He must be wrong. No self-respecting shark would be out on a night like this. Maybe he ought to tell Mike, but, if he was wrong, the statement would only add to his brother's worries. Having, in his logical way, decided to drop the whole thing he was completely unprepared when his legs were brushed again! Without thinking, he kicked the unknown thing and felt his heel hit a sold, unrelenting object.

This sudden movement brought a "What's wrong with you?" from Mike. Without answering, Rich flipped his body over and gave the offending object a vicious push. There followed a slight experimental skirmish, then a cry of delight.

"Mike," Rich bellowed at the top of his lungs, "It's a log!"

"Where are you?" asked Mike. "A what?"

"A log, a good ole log," yelled Rich. "Hurry and get on it."

Mike appeared confused for a moment but indicated understanding by swimming toward his brother. He celebrated the discovery of the log with a wild whoop of joy and playfully pitched some water into Rich's face.

"Now I know we have it made," said Mike. His tone indicated all his happiness in this wonderful discovery.

"Thanks, God," whispered Rich below his breath, "I knew you weren't really mad."

Even though the magnitude of their peril had not lessened much, the log restored their confidence in their ability to survive. The great piece of wood had become a floating, bouncing ally. Rich tried to straddle the log and ride it, but soon gave up his efforts when he felt the chilling results of the wind on his wet body. It was much warmer and even more comfortable in the warm tropical water.

Mike grinned at Rich's attempt at levity and then decided to reevaluate the situation. The log must be some factor from which he could determine something. Since it seemed void of barnacles and solid, this would indicate that it had been in the water only a short time. It had been impossible to determine in which direction it had been floating, but somehow he trusted in his reasoning that the direction of the storm was blowing them toward land. If this was correct, the log was a welcome companion. In this situation, it was a comfort regardless of its destination.

For some time, Mike let his mind rest and body relax. He kept his eyes focused on his little brother. He was becoming tired and knew that Rich must likewise feel the discomfort of fatigue. It would soon be light enough so that they could see their salvation or their doom. He changed positions to relieve his cramped muscles and resigned himself to the wild motions of the log.

He must have dozed for a moment for he snapped awake with an instant loss of memory as to his whereabouts. Frantically, he checked his hold on the log and scanned its length for his brother. He was gone!

CHAPTER 3 - LOST

This horrible discovery shocked him into a frantic series of screams for his brother. His only answer was the nasal moan of the wind. He attempted to swim in circles around the log and ceased this effort when a large wave almost threw the log on his back. The impossible hopelessness of the situation hit him with all of its nastiness. What could he do?

He tried calling again until he felt hysteria creep into his voice. Then a great calm seized him. It was a calm saturated with thoughts and images of his brother floating lifelessly in the great sea. He felt the warm tears from his eyes and it was only with extraordinary effort that he managed to regain some control of his emotions. Deep down in his soul, he knew that Rich was a survivor.

"He's not dead," he moaned. "Rich isn't dead."

His despair reflected itself in the tone of his statement but he struggled within himself to believe it. He knew he had to master his confusion or he would completely go to pieces. There had to be something he could do. But, what?

Disorganized thoughts and worry for his brother crowded into his mind, but would linger only long enough to confuse him. The constant pounding of the waves and wind had dulled his reflexes and his ability to concentrate. He was so numb that for a moment he did not realize that something was happening contrary to this horrible wet environment and the loss of his brother. His feet touched a sandy bottom.

When the realization of this phenomenon finally dawned upon him, he felt no elation and for a moment stood dumbly staring into the waves until he was smashed from his feet by a large wave. Suddenly his wits returned and he immediately pushed the log away from him realizing that it was best to discard this companion before it became a deadly hindrance in the surf. It seemed like miles of stumbling, swimming, and crawling elapsed before he finally dragged his body ashore and collapsed on the beach. The sea was reluctant to release such a promising victim.

Mike finally dragged himself away from the clutching surf and from shear exhaustion, curled up on the dry beach and slept. His sleep was troubled by intermittent dreams, but his body refused to awaken until its rest requirements had been fulfilled. This took about four or more hours when he awoke to a dreary, damp dawn. He was cold, hungry, and utterly miserable. He studied the length of the beach in both directions, but other than the normal storm debris, it was deserted.

Behind him was a jungle with the scrub, vine-infested trees sloping away from the sea pushed by the prevailing wind. He was undecided whether to chase the forlorn hope of walking the beach in search of Rich or somehow work on the possibility of starting a fire. The latter seemed more practical so he dragged himself into the protection of the trees.

The pangs of hunger and thirst seized him but he realized that warmth was necessary and his wants would have to be fulfilled in some orderly routine. He soon satisfied his thirst from a hollow in an old stump, which had rotted

17

away into a natural bowl. It took him almost an hour to locate and tear away a proper and flexible limb from which he intended to make a bow to start an Indian fire. He tried to use a vine as a string but soon gave this idea up and reluctantly tore a piece from the hem of his water-soaked shirt and twisted it into a rope.

Then he wandered among the many trees and dark undergrowth looking for some material to use as tinder and a block of wood to start the fire on. The search seemed in vain because everything was wet or completely waterlogged. He sat down to rest and noticed that the ground was rising sharply toward a rocky hill. After a short rest, he moved toward the hill to determine its possibility as a lookout point. He entered a small clearing which afforded him a clear view of a sheer wall of eroded rock. It was exceedingly high but if he could climb to the top, its summit would certainly be a vantage point to look around the surrounding country. After a more careful scrutiny of the rock wall in front of him, he thought he could make out the foggy outline of a cave. At least it was some sort of indentation in the rock wall that could afford some protection from the weather.

He trudged toward the rise with more purpose in his stride for his discovery opened up many useful opportunities. He could not only set up some sort of protected headquarters but he would soon be able to scan the beach for some sign of Rich. The last thought quickened his pace but due to his weakened condition, he soon settled back to a brisk walk. Suddenly, he came upon a path that headed toward his intended destination. He noted that there was no evidence that the path had been used recently. Leaves, twigs, and vines littered the path. The only footprints he could see in the muted light were those of small animals and birds.

With a sense of excitement, he followed the path easily and confirmed that either it headed near or directly to the opening he had just spotted. Within five minutes, he could recognize that what he had seen was really a cave and with a sudden burst of speed was soon at its gaping mouth.

He stood on a broad, flat rock shelf that extended slightly beyond the face of the cliff and faced the beach. He anxiously let his eyes sweep the sandy shore but unfortunately, could only see a small section close to the water's edge. His restricted observation only resulted in a sickening feeling in his stomach. There was still no sign of Rich.

Though he was unhappy by not seeing Rich, he decided he had better make a quick inspection of the cave and get on with his attempt to start a fire. He carefully made his way through the entrance and discovered that the interior was light. Glancing upward, he saw that there was an opening, which angled to the top of the hill. Even though the light coming through the shaft was poor now, it gave the interior a cozy atmosphere and the natural ventilation it afforded had kept the cave dry.

His eyes soon adjusted to the dim light. He scoured the large room with his eyes and noted an assorted group of objects in one corner. His heart raced in the anticipation of what he would find and with a bound, he was upon the objects like a small boy at Christmas time.

CHAPTER 4 - TREASURES

There were three wooden boxes, a hatchet, two saws, some coils of rope, a small stack of wood, and a whole group of items neatly placed on a crudely built shelf attached to the side of the cave. A careful check of the shelf's contents revealed pieces of sheet metal, assorted tools, two boxes of matches, a pan, an iron skillet, and miscellaneous tin cans filled with nails and random pieces of metal.

Discontinuing his search in order to fulfill his more urgent need for warmth, he gathered some small kindling scattered about the floor and struck one of the matches. The head immediately disintegrated. He tried another with the same result. Realizing then that he would have to dry the matches first, he painstakingly rubbed several of the matches on a piece of dry rope. After two failures, he finally struck the third match and happily started his first fire in this strange and unfamiliar land.

He fed the struggling fire with larger and larger pieces of wood he found stacked in the cave and soon felt the first comfort he had in many hours. As the strength and courage seemed to return to every part of his body, he finally picked up the hatchet and attacked one of the boxes with gusto. Within seconds, he had removed the lid and found to his joy that he was the possessor of cans and cans of soup. Noting that the cans were in excellent condition, he tore one open with the hatchet and gulped it down greedily. It was the most wonderful thing he had ever tasted.

He opened another but warmed it first over the fire before he slowly consumed its contents with little gasps of contentment. He completely relaxed for a time and would have dropped off to sleep if the unshakable depression over Rich's disappearance had not forced him to his feet. He wanted to explore the cave and its surroundings, but he could not do this until he searched the beach once more for his brother.

Grasping the hatchet, he left the cave after making certain that he banked the fire with plenty of wood to make sure it would not go out and everything else was ship-shape. The descent to the beach took only ten minutes since the path he had previously discovered went almost in a straight line to that destination. The rain had stopped and the wind was blowing itself out in fitful gusts. Glancing at the sky and thinning cloud cover, he guessed that the sun would be out by the following day.

He started down the beach with the wind slightly at his back knowing that this was the only practical direction in which to look. As he was blown downwind onto the beach, so would Rich have been blown in that direction?

He wandered along the water's edge for two hours finding nothing but the normal refuge cast up by the surf. Eventually the beach bent itself into a small bay, which presented the fact that he was on a peninsula with the possibility that the body of land he was on was an island. However, he could not recall any island along the coast of this size and decided that he may be on the mainland somewhere in the unexplored jungle area south of Talanka. He stood on the tip of the peninsula for some time trying to decide whether to continue his search or return to the cave. He finally concluded that he would go back to the cave since he would have to renew his search on the opposite side of the small bay due to the direction of the storm's harsh winds. Such an excursion would require some preparation because it would take at least four days. He sadly retraced his steps to the cave in the hill. He realized that somehow he must rid himself of this depressed feeling and attempt to control his thinking to only positive planning.

The first thing he decided to do was to start a large fire on the outside ledge of the cave as a signal for any passing boat or Rich. He would light it at night since it could be seen for many miles at sea and he was certain there was or would be some sort of search organized to find he and Rich. He soon accomplished the task of dragging large pieces of wood to the ledge and even though it was still wet, he decided the dry wood in the cave would give the pyre a sufficient start to result in a large and merry fire.

He made his way to the top of the hill, which was about forty yards above him. Except for a few places where the rock rubble made progress a little difficult, he had little trouble reaching the summit. From this vantage point, he surveyed his surroundings. He scanned the beach and estimated that he could see about five miles along the water's edge before the trees blocked his view. Back of him was jungle that seemed to become less impenetrable as he looked deeper into its depths. He saw and heard many birds he was familiar with from his long stay at the plantation. For an instant, he caught a glimpse of a large animal slinking across the edge of a small opening. It occurred to him that the fire on the ledge would now have a two-fold purpose and he must give some thought to creating a weapon of some sort for protection and hunting. He could not live on soup forever.

He lingered on the peak a while longer letting his eyes slowly sweep the countryside and then returned to the cave. He busied himself for some time exploring the cave and found two separate tunnels, which appeared to disappear into the hill. He decided they would stand to be investigated later since there were more immediate problems at hand. He made a comfortable bed-mat on the floor of the cave from moss and palms from the nearby trees, then replenished his woodpile. Next, he stacked and checked all of the supplies and tools. It was not too long before he felt that everything within the cave was well organized. Luckily, he had found some rusty fishing hooks in an old can and was pleased that with a little work he could put together a crude but serviceable fishing rig.

Noting that it would soon be dark, he realized he was thirsty. He made a quick trip to the hollow stump and found that most of the water was gone. He was able to quench his thirst but knew that he must locate a reliable source of water the following day. He returned to the cave and prepared himself a can of soup, which he drank slowly and with pleasure. Even though his hunger demanded more nourishment, he refrained from the desire to open another can. He must watch his supplies carefully until he could acquire other sources of food from the sea or jungle.

He lit the fire outside the cave, even though it might be a little early, because he was uncertain how well the wet wood would burn. This accomplished, he returned to the cave and decided he would spend some time making a spearhead from the scrap metal. Three hours later he had finally created a crude resemblance to a spear head by beating the metal into its shape with the back of the axe's head and a large stone imbedded in the cave's floor. He was not thoroughly satisfied with the results, but felt more secure with the metal spearhead in his hand. He would attach it to a shaft in the morning and planned to try his hand at some small metal tips for arrows. He felt certain he could construct a serviceable bow and some arrows with which he could possibly bag some small game.

After building up both fires with more fuel, he decided to get some sleep so he could arise at the crack of dawn and prepare himself for a better search for his brother. Even in his worried condition, he soon fell into a deep slumber clouded only by confused dreams. In his dreams, he relived the horrible experience of the storm and his eventual deliverance from the sea to the shoreline. For a time the dreams left him and then returned by placing him in a strange jungle full of large snakes. He dreamed that he was surrounded and one of the snakes flung itself upon him and was attempting to strangle him with it powerful coils.

His eyes snapped open and for a moment and he was released from that horrible predicament. Just as the full power of his sense returned and he realized it had all been just a nightmare, he suddenly felt something touch his back.

CHAPTER 5 – FOUND

His first impulse was to jump, but somehow he managed to remain perfectly still. The thing, whatever it was, left for a second then returned with an exploratory search at the nape of his neck and shoulders. His mind was flying like a rocket attempting to plan his next action and his eyes frantically searched for some sort of weapon within close reach. He spotted a piece of firewood and decided that he would spring to his feet, grab this crude weapon and face this unknown intruder.

He was frightened to the point of paralysis, but knew he had to combat this venomous intruder or he could die a horrible and slow death from a poisonous snakebite. He knew from previous experiences with snakes that any sudden move could trigger an immediate defensive reaction by the snake that could bury its fangs into his neck or back. Mike also knew that his warmth was an attractor to the cold-blooded viper that might consider him prey. One way or the other, he had to rid the cave of this threat.

He waited for several minutes until the mysterious thing ceased its blood chilling probing of his neck. He sprang away from his sleeping mat and to his feet, brushing away the touch of the viper, and with a swift and accurate motion, grabbed the weapon he required. He then quickly turned to face his enemy.

It was Rich!

CHAPTER 6 - RELIEF

For a surprised and baffled second, Mike stood in his crouched, defensive position with the piece of wood in his hand and gazed upon his grinning brother standing there like a ghost with a piece of rope in his hand. Then with a cry full of relief and joy, he leapt upon his brother and hugged him as if he were going to disappear any moment.

"How in the world did you get here?" questioned Mike.

"Have you got anything to eat?" evaded Rich. "I'm starving!"

Without further ado, Mike opened two cans of the soup and set them on the fire. Due to Rich's impatient hunger, one can was barely lukewarm before he grabbed it and gulped it down much like Mike had done on his first day in the cave. After he consumed the second can, Rich requested some vanilla ice cream, but finally agreed to skip the humor and tell the impatient Mike of his adventures.

"I must have fallen asleep," began Rich, "because I woke up spitting out half the ocean. I was about twenty yards from the log. I could still see it, when the granddaddy of all waves picked me up and must have carried me thirty or forty yards more before I could unscramble myself. I tried to swim back toward the log, even though I couldn't see it, but gave up because the waves were too much for me. I finally got back to floating again and in about an hour I was washed onto the beach. I must have run five miles up and down the shore looking for you, but finally had to get under the trees of the jungle and get some sleep because I was pooped."

Mike commented, "I must have run right by you while you were sleeping. I did the same thing you did."

"I woke up some time this morning," continued Rich, "about to freeze to death and thirsty as the dickens. I finally found a puddle of water and felt better even though I expected to get sick from drinking the mess. I walked up and down the beach for a while then headed back into the jungle. That's where I stumbled onto a wild fruit tree. After eating everything I could hold, I did a little exploring and spotted this hill. I was heading back to the beach when I heard a noise like a waterfall. I immediately tried to locate it, but got a little lost. I finally found the source of the noise and it was a small waterfall on a tiny creek not very far from here. After messing around in the pool at the bottom of the waterfall for quite some time, I tried to start a fire with some rocks. I got some sparks from the rocks, but never could get a fire going. I did find some delicious mussels and a frog near the waterfall. I couldn't make myself eat the frog without cooking it, but the mussels were delicious."

Rich hesitated for a moment while he added some wood to the fire, rubbing himself with contentment, and stated, "Boy, this feels good." Then with a little shyness in his voice he asked, "Say, Mike, do you reckon we could afford another can of soup?"

Mike laughed and immediately opened two cans with the admission that this was going to be a celebration, even though he felt it was probably against his better judgement.

After consuming the warm soup, Rich continued his story when Mike insisted. "Well, anyway, I started out for this hill again and was almost here when I ran into a big wild boar and barely made it up a tree. That darn critter hung around for hours, and every time I thought he was gone, I would start to crawl down from my perch only to have that ham-hock come charging toward me. Evidently he finally did take off because I got down to the ground and ran like a scared rabbit to a small opening in the rocks somewhere on the other side of this hill. Even though I was about to freeze to death, I decided to try sleeping there."

"I must have dozed off for a couple of hours because when I wakened here I could see the light from your fire. All I could think of was cannibals or headhunters so, even though I was curious, I stayed in my little hole and tried to sleep. Guess I must have slept some but don't know for how long because the next thing I knew I was awake, cold, and utterly miserable. I looked over the hill and there was the light from your doggone fire, just begging me to come over."

"Well, I finally did and here I am, and please don't get mad at me for playing the trick on you with the rope."

"Boy, you sure gave me a miserable time for a spell," admitted Mike, "but forget it and let's get some sleep. I bet your bushed."

"Wait a minute," said Rich, "how about telling me how you got here?"

"Let's save it till morning," answered Mike, "and, then I'll catch you up on all the details."

Rich shrugged his shoulders to admit it was a good idea and, after stacking some more wood on the fire, they stretched out on the makeshift pallet-bed and fell happily asleep.

CHAPTER 7 – PREPARATIONS

In the following days, the boys kept themselves busy making spears, bows, and arrows. They set snares, fished, and gathered fruit. They did all the things necessary for their existence and security. Whenever there was an opportunity, they searched the sea for signs of a ship. Only once did they imagine that they saw one. If it was a ship, it was so far off they were not sure it could even see their signal fire. They continued with the chores that seemed to have become a fixed routine in their new lives.

Mike had long since informed Rich of his adventures from the log to their reunion and it was not long before the hardships of the storm had faded from their minds. They tried to piece together the origin of the mysterious cache they had discovered in the cave. They talked and wondered about what happened to the person or persons who had lived there. Since there were practically no clues, they eventually gave this detective work up and just felt a sense of gratitude that they had been so fortunate.

They had spent most of one day thoroughly exploring the cave and discovered that one of the tunnels extended through the hill with an opening to the opposite side. The opening was located on a perpendicular cliff with a sheer drop of about twenty-five feet to the jungle floor. They constructed a crude but serviceable ladder out of small trees and vines. Access to and from this opening would save them many steps when they were foraging in this area. They would no longer have to hike completely around the rocky hill to gain access to this backside area that contained plentiful fruit trees and small game. They referred to this entrance as the "back door" and the main mouth of the cave as their "front door."

The boys practiced many hours a day with their weapons and soon became extremely proficient with their use. Mike had developed a tolerable accuracy with his spear, which made him deadly at ten to twenty yards. Even though he was good with his bow, he could never match Rich's uncanny ability with this weapon. Rich seemed to have some inborn instinct of judgement with his bow that mystified even himself. He bagged several crane-like birds, which they roasted over their fire and gave them a break from their diet of fish and fruit.

Even though their snares had yielded only one edible animal, a small pig, they developed a sense of security as far as food and water were concerned. They talked casually of attempting to walk north through the jungle to Talanka. This idea began to grow into a definite set of plans as each passing day revealed less and less chances for a rescue. The first part of their plan was to strike out further into the jungle to test their weapons on larger game and to experiment with their abilities to adapt themselves to the dangers that lurked there.

After much discussion, they finally decided to equip themselves with three days of supplies and live in the jungle for that period of time. The boys estimated they could make about thirty miles in the three days and would attempt to swing in a wide circle and return to the cave on the fourth day. After the experience gained from this expedition, they would then finalize their plans and attempt to walk to the nearest point of civilization that they encountered.

For one full day, they worked feverishly to pack, but discarded things from their packs since they knew they had to travel light. Rich wanted to take everything, but finally gave in to Mike's patient explanations and reluctantly discarded useless items, one at a time, until his load was about fifteen pounds. By nightfall, they were completely prepared and after a particularly heavy meal, they immediately went to bed so they could be on their way at sunrise.

The excitement of their venture resulted in a night of catnaps and both decided to abandon their attempts at sleep when the first light appeared in the east. They built up their signal fire and prepared themselves a tasteless breakfast. They then waited for over an hour until the sun eventually smiled at them over the treetops. With excited steps, they raced down the hill and headed into the jungle in a southeasterly direction.

CHAPTER 8 - TREKKING

For approximately three hours, the boys walked into the ever-thickening jungle. Wherever possible, Mike would mark their trail with the hatchet and Rich would break branches on the small trees and underbrush. They did this only as a precaution in case they had to retrace their steps in a hurry, though they did not intend to return on this route.

The going was easy initially, and they gradually relaxed to the soft feel of the mysterious jungle. They kept their weapons ready for any sudden emergency. Their knowledge of the jungle was limited, even though both boys had been on occasional hunting trips with their father in the dense forests and grassy plains near their plantation. They were familiar with the necessary awareness and caution that must be maintained for poisonous vipers and the dreaded constrictors. The boys' eyes were also in constant search for the giant scorpions and the detested tsetse flies, which seemed to be created to make their lives miserable. The present multitudes of stinging insects had to be ignored as a way of life. Both boys knew that the real dangers in this wild and untamed land were the small things and not particularly the large animals, which the inexperienced considered their primary danger. They knew that the larger beasts avoided humans unless hunger or other unusual conditions existed that caused them to ignore their natural repugnance to humans.

The boys accidentally found a well-defined animal trail, which to the best of their reckoning, was headed almost due east. Since there was no real purpose in continuing on their present route, they decided to follow the trail. It seemed to afford the least amount of obstacles. Mike suggested a rest before continuing and both boys immediately dumped their packs and relaxed against two giant trees. Quietly, they enjoyed the noisy peace of the jungle that hummed and buzzed with a variety of soft sounds.

Rich went to sleep immediately. Mike gazed upon his brother with an amused smile. The torn and tattered clothes he wore exposed his muscular frame and even in his peaceful slumber, he created the picture of a dynamo of wiry strength. Rich was going to be a tall and powerful man with a well-proportioned chest and slim long legs. The only strange thing about his build was the unusual size of his strong arms, which had developed beyond his years. They were well proportioned but were somehow out of scale with the rest of his body. Mike knew of the terrific strength of his brother's body since it had become gradually more difficult to handle him in their playful wrestling matches.

Mike realized that it would not be many years before the wrestling matches would be very even and possibly in Rich's favor. He guessed he outweighed Rich by fifteen or twenty pounds and topped him in height by a couple of inches. He was not aware of his own powerfully built body and had accepted his great strength merely because of the many hours of swimming and exercising he had donated to it. He decided that he and Rich were exceptionally fortunate regardless of their present situation and felt with great confidence that they would soon be united with their parents.

CHAPTER 9 – THE JUNGLE

Mike reluctantly awakened Rich and with some amount of grumbling on Rich's part, they started down the trail to where it might lead. The trail was gradually sloping downward into a valley and the vegetation was thickening so rapidly that it seemed to threaten the existence of their found animal trail at any moment. Except for a few places, the diluted rays of the sun were a dull, twilight tone that made it difficult to see the obstacles jutting into the trail.

The jungle birds could be heard high overhead along with the invisible chatter of the small monkeys. The boys had slowed their pace not only due to the increased difficulties encountered on the trail but also because they sensed the need for extra caution. At one spot, Mike stopped suddenly and leaning back, pushed his hand into Rich's chest. With a nod of his head, he indicated that something was on the trail ahead.

"Snake," he whispered, never taking his eyes from the serpent that lay coiled only feet in front of them.

For a moment, neither the snake nor the boys moved. Then the snake made a slow and deliberate move with its head that the boys interpreted as an intention of attack. The twang of the two bowstrings was simultaneous and they both jumped backward as the writing body of the huge reptile thrashed about the ground.

"Got him," breathed Rich.

"Careful," cautioned Mike, holding Rich back with one hand.

Both were ready for a second shot but it was soon apparent that they had mortally wounded the snake as its body slowly ceased its wild curling movements. They crept cautiously forward and saw that both arrows had speared the snake's head. Mike extracted their arrows and cleaned them with leaves while Rich kept his bow and an arrow ready for other dangers. They said nothing, but within each of them was born a great sense of confidence. They had made their first defensive kill!

Stepping around the quivering body, they continued down the trail with a backward glance at their victim. Both were immensely pleased with themselves and felt a true sense of security that had only been an untried ability when they left the cave. They also were aware that if there was one snake on this trail, there could be many more.

Their eyes became accustomed to the poor light and they noted with relief that the trail was becoming slightly wider but in turn, there was more and more evidence of swampy land ahead. Small patches of water and cypress trees were becoming more prevalent. For several hours they trudged toward the floor of the valley until weariness and hunger made them search for a place to rest and eat. Fortunately, they came upon a small hill that slanted away from the trail and was partially clear of underbrush. This would give them a vantage point from which to observe the surrounding country and provide a welcome relief from the sticky heat and humidity of the jungle valley.

Wearily they finally reached the top of the hill and were briefly surprised by the sudden departure of a pygmy antelope, which scampered away into the forest. After a short rest, Rich started a small fire with the fire-bow they had constructed at the cave while Mike opened two cans of their precious soup and placed some papaws fruit on his pack to complete their frugal meal.

"Man I wished we had some of Mom's homemade cornbread!" commented Rich. Mike just nodded in agreement, as he continued to stir the soup. The hot soup restored their energy and the sweet taste of the papaws temporarily satisfied their hunger. Rich issued a slight complaint about the many seeds in the jungle fruit, but devoured every morsel. "We should have skinned that snake and cooked him," was Rich's suggestion for a main course.

"You are probably right," replied Mike, "But, I'm not real sure if it was poisonous or not. Better safe than sorry out here in the jungle. Wait here, I'll be right back."

Mike spotted a convenient climbing tree from which to observe the area from, and after climbing as high as he could, gazed out on the landscape. To the north and east he could see nothing but a limitless expanse of huge trees. He figured that much of what he could see was more swampland due to the visible groups of cypress trees ahead of them. He estimated that they were not more than one-half mile from the marshes and could detect the existence of a small river about two miles east of the hill. Through this gnarled mass of vegetation, he and Rich would have to find their way since it was time that they started in a northerly or at least a northeasterly direction in order to return to their cave.

The hill that they were on was evidently part of a mountain range that he could see far to the southeast. Mike's view was partially blocked in this direction but he noticed that the jungle seemed to surrender itself to a great expanse of plains that probably extended into the foothills of the mountains. It was difficult to judge distances due to a haze that hung in patches over the jungle, but he guessed that the mountains were at least twenty to twenty-five miles away.

To the west, the direction from which they had come, he could see very little but typical jungle forests with massive trees that extended over the top of the hill. He climbed down and after relating his observations to Rich, he suggested that it might be wise to spend the night where they were.

"That swamp will be murder at night," Mike said, "and we better try to get through it during the day. I don't think we could make it now even though we have about six hours until sundown."

"Sure would like to fish that river," commented Rich, "but maybe we could get a bird or something to eat tonight."

"Let's get further away from the game trail and then we'll see what we can find," suggested Mike.

CHAPTER 10 – THE HUNT

They immediately broke camp and continued along the crown of the hill for about a half a mile until they came upon a small spring. This clean clear water decided the location of their new camp for the night and Rich built a fire using a glowing limb from their luncheon campfire.

For a time they discussed the possibility of sleeping in a tree but after much discussion it was decided they would stand alternate guard and trust that the fire would discourage any unfriendly prowlers. As a matter of caution, a close and convenient tree was selected which was to be their refuge in case of an emergency.

After they were satisfied with the camp preparations, the boys grabbed their bows and arrows and started down the hill toward the edge of the swamp. From the noise that surrounded them as they came to the base of the hill, it was apparent that they were near the nesting grounds of thousands of different birds. Cautiously they crept forward and established a position behind a tangle of bushes and vines that camouflaged their presence but gave them an excellent vantage point to spot any stray game.

They had not long to wait. The swamp was alive with flashing colors as the multitude of smaller birds nervously fluttered from tree to tree and the larger cranes casually waded along the shoreline in search of food. Rich nudged Mike and with a nod of his head, indicated two large cranes that had wandered within ten yards of their hiding place. He rubbed his stomach and licked his lips to show his anticipation of the forthcoming feast. Each boy selected his target and let their arrows fly at the same instant. Their aim was true and the two hunters, with satisfied grins on their faces retrieved their kills amid the confusion and alarmed cries of the escaping hordes of birds.

They plucked, cleaned, and placed the cranes over their small campfire on a spit. While the birds were cooking, the boys made a successful search for fruits and berries. They even found some wild onions that they stuffed into the cavities of the two birds, along with some of the berries. Soon the meal was ready and both boys enjoyed the taste of the seasoned birds immensely. Later, they both admitted to each other that the birds looked much better than they tasted.

They decided that on the next day to follow the river as long as possible since the traveling would probably be much easier than through the swamp. Mike suggested that he hoped to hit high ground the following day that might open the possibility of bagging a reedbuck, or some other type of antelope or deer. They could use the skin for many purposes and their desire for the taste of meat was becoming acute.

After a long day of following the river, they made camp again as the evening approached. Their meal consisted of leftover crane meat and some additional berries and fruit they had collected along the way.

They each made a soft pallet of palms and moss to sleep on next to their campfire, and enjoyed an attractive view of the sunset falling behind the mountains in the west. It was pleasant to discuss the many uses they proposed to use the imaginary deer skins but soon Rich's yawning indicated the necessity of sleep. Mike volunteered for the first watch with very little argument from Rich, and soon his light snoring indicated his complete surrender to weariness.

CHAPTER 11 – ONWARD

Except for the distant sounds of jungle beasts and an occasional pair of curious eyes that would appear on the edge of the fire light, the night was uneventful. At sunrise, the boys prepared a fast meal from the evenings' leftovers and were once again walking along the river's edge.

For several hours, they followed the casual meanderings of the river making occasional detours wherever the underbrush and heavy grasses impeded their path. It was an exciting journey for they saw many crocodiles, two huge boa snakes, and many different types of monkeys and water fowl. They also saw a small herd of swamp deer grazing near the opposite side of the river but they were too far to shoot at them. They discovered many different animal tracks along the edge of the river, but other than to increase their vigilance and stealth, the boys ignored the presence of these dangers and made excellent time through the dense vegetation.

When the sun was over their head, about noon, they stopped and Rich tried his hand at fishing. Mike climbed another high tree near the stream to investigate their route for the afternoon. Far to the north, he spotted small hills, which indicated the possibility of reaching higher land, and possibly savanna country late in the day. He noted that the river was definitely turning toward the east and it would be necessary to veer away from its banks within the next hour. With a little luck, they might be out of the dense jungle in a couple of hours that would greatly help their progress. Satisfied with the outlook, Mike descended from the tree and went in search of Rich. He soon found him with a sizable catch of fish and practically had to force him away from this haven of sport. It took both of them to carry the huge catch of fish that Rich so proficiently acquired.

After cooking and smoking the huge catch of fish Rich had provided, they were on the move again. They saved many of the cooked fish for their evening meal. As they headed away from the river the path became much rougher and at times it appeared that forward progress would be impossible. However, by using many detours and at times hacking away the tangled and reluctant undergrowth, they eventually advanced out of the ooze of the swamp.

From then on, their route became much easier. The thick vegetation of the swamp gradually surrendered itself to a great, park like forest with little undergrowth, tall trees, and a soft trail to follow. This beautiful timberland rejuvenated their lagging spirits and created much bantering talk between the two brothers. In this light-hearted mood, they increased their pace for several hours until they came across a small, crystal-clear stream that was lined with beautiful light green ferns. There was no debate. Here they decided to rest. They were still in a carefree mood, so they snacked on some of the left over fish and local wild fruit.

They enjoyed this beautiful paradise for the better part of an hour before they decided it was time to hit the trail again. They headed upstream, since the stream was flowing from the direction they were headed, the boys happily followed its course. It was a pleasant hike. The small stream maintained a fairly straight course and the boys stopped frequently to quench their thirst and playfully splashed each other with its waters.

The further they progressed up the stream, the more they noticed that the forest was thinning and yielded to country that was more open. This verified Mike's opinion of the possibility of plains or prairies at the foot of the hills. The stream had decreased to a rivulet and suddenly headed out toward the hills to the east, which was probably its place of origin. Since there only remained about two hours of daylight, the boys determined to make camp in a small cluster of trees near this small water source.

"I would guess that we are about twelve to fifteen miles from the cave which ought to be in that direction," said Mike pointing in a southwesterly direction.

"Boy, that's a lot of walking," stated Rich, "but I'll be glad to get there…my feet are barking like a hyena."

"We ought to make it in about six or seven hours if we don't hit any rough stuff," suggested Mike.

"It couldn't be any worse that the junk we have been through," remarked Rich.

"I'm not sure you have noticed some of the tracks we have seen next to the stream, but I have a hunch we are on the edge of lion country. We're going to have to watch it," stated Mike.

"Lions!" exclaimed Rich.

"Ah, don't worry, Rich," returned Mike, "their not as tough as everyone thinks. We'll just have to watch ourselves."

With a shrug of his strong shoulders, Rich indicated his lack of confidence in this statement and then as if to change the subject he proposed, "I'll try to get some fish, if you'll start a fire."

"Good for you dear brother," said Mike. "Happy fishing, and don't wander off too far."

Rich found some grubs under a small rotten tree that had fallen near the stream and was soon tempting whatever fish happened to be in the small pool below the campsite. His luck held out and even though the fish were small, he soon returned with a sufficient batch for dinner that evening. Mike's small campfire was perfect for cooking the fish on small sticks angled into the fire.

"I'm starting to grow gills," commented Rich. "I've eaten so many darn fish; I'd be surprised if I didn't have gills and a dorsal fin on my back!"

Mike just smiled and commented, "Better than nothing, right?"

They both stopped talking. "Did you hear that?" asked Rich.

"Yep," replied Mike. "Sure looks like we are in lion country now."

CHAPTER 12 – DANGER

Mike and Rich both heard the roars of multiple lions. The beasts were several miles away, but could easily cover that distance quickly if they knew the brothers were there.

"What do you think we should do, Mike?" asked Rich. "Run or fight?"

Mike was thinking the same thing that Rich was thinking that they had two choices: Grab their packs and head as quickly as they could away from the lions and toward their cave home, or build a large fire and wait for the lions to find them. The first option seemed much smarter, but the risk they would have is if the lions saw them running across the prairie and caught them in the open terrain. Building a fire would just draw the lions to them quicker and all they had were a spear and their bows and arrows to fend off one or more three hundred pound cats that were lethal and efficient killers.

"Rich, I think we better get the heck out of here. We are fortunate that we have a decent moon to see with tonight and if we get moving now, we might be able to stay ahead of the lions until we reach some tall trees. What do you think?"

"I think I am already on my way," smiled Rich as he quickly put on his pack and started to walk away.

"Hang on a minute, Rich. Let's kill this campfire and spread the fish we have caught here. If they come this direction, then maybe they will fill up on our fish and not want to chase us down."

"Good idea, Mike. You douse the fire and I will get all the fish out and spread them around on the ground."

Both the boys moved as if they were on fire. In just a moment, Mike had doused the small campfire and spread its ashes and Rich took the many fish he had caught and spread them about the campsite to cover their scent and provide food to the lions, if they came to investigate. "Okay," said Mike. "Let's get a move on it."

The boys were in excellent shape and now that they were in an area where there were few trees and no jungle, they started to run toward their cave. They knew if they walked at the pace they had been walking, it would take five or six hours to get back to their cave. At their jogging rate, it would take them less than two hours. Depending on how interested the lions were in them, their fish, or any other game the lions might be hunting, that might give them enough time to reach the safety of their cave.

They knew, however, there was one problem with their cave. There was no way to close off the mouth of the cave from the lions if they followed the boys back there. They could only hope they had left enough fish to slow them down, and the lions would decide to go another direction.

CHAPTER 13 – PURSUIT

It took about an hour to reach the first sizeable trees and they could tell that the fish had not satisfied the lions. The roars were getting closer and more frequent as the boys jogged on for their lives. The lions seemed to spreading out on the prairie trying to surround the boys.

"Mike," Rich puffed, "I think the cats are on our trail."

"Yea, it looks like we may have to climb a tree and wait them out."

Thanks to sufficient moonlight, they could see a tall straight tree several hundred yards ahead with multiple lower limbs that would be easy to climb, but the thought in their heads was, "do lions like to climb trees?" Neither Mike nor Rich had studied about lions. Every time they had seen lions on television or during their trips to Africa, they were sleeping together in their prides in tall grass on the ground. They both hoped that these were lazy, ground hugging lions, and not athletic tree-climbing lions.

Once they got to the tree, Rich scooted up like one of the monkeys they had been watching and Mike was right behind him. They each found a large and relatively comfortable limb to sit on forty or fifty feet off the ground. They no sooner settled in the tree and two lionesses raced by the tree they were hiding in and kept going. They did not stop. It had not even dawned on the boys that the lions might not see them climb up into the tree. Unfortunately, the two lions turned quickly around and ran up to the base of their tree.

Their cold yellow eyes looked up and directly at Mike and Rich clinging to their branches. It was obvious that the lions were tracking the boys by scent and when they did not smell them anymore, the lions knew that they needed to turn around. The downward movement of cooler nighttime air blew the boy's scent to the lions, so the predators knew exactly where the boys were. The lions continued to look up into the tree and licked their lips.

"Mike. Mike. I don't like the way that lion is licking its mouth. It reminds me too much of the way I was licking my lips before we shot those two cranes."

"I agree. Maybe we can dissuade them from trying to climb the tree. See if you can break off a large branch from the tree. We will use that to throw at them or poke them if they try to climb. I still have my spear and we both have our bows and arrows. They might not kill the lions, but it sure might discourage them from trying to eat us. Get ready."

They threw their branches at the lions, but with no success. Of course, these were not lazy ground-hugging lions. These were Olympian lions and they loved to climb trees.

Fortunately, for the boys, they could only do this one at a time because of the size of the tree, which was to the boy's advantage. The first and largest female lion rose up on its hind legs placing its front paws on the trunk of the tree, extracted its claws from its front paws, and then slowly and carefully ascended the tree, while watching each of the boys. She had no problem getting up about ten feet off the ground and to the first cross branch, but she hesitated there. The boys did not understand what she was doing, but it soon became clear that she had stopped to encourage her pride chum to come up as well. The second smaller lion also began to climb the trunk of the tree, planning to obtain a rest on an opposite branch to the other lion.

"Mike, I think these ladies are a team," commented Rich. "I also think they want to invite us to dinner, and we are the dinner."

"Yep. Are you ready?" asked Mike. Rich grunted that he was. "Okay, let's let 'em have it."

The twangs of their bowstrings were simultaneous. Mike's arrow went into the side of the lion standing on the branch, and Rich's arrow went into the forehead of the second lion climbing up the trunk of the tree. Both lions let out a massive roar and fell from the tree. The lion with the arrow in its side, ran off into the dense grass near where they had come from, and the other lion lay twitching at the bottom of the tree. Apparently, thanks to Rich's strength and bow, his arrow had penetrated the lion's head and killed it instantly. They could hear the lion Mike had shot twitching and tearing up the long grass she had run into. She was in her death throes as well. Just like that, the hunted had become the hunters.

"Mike. Can you believe that?" yelled Rich, "We killed two lions. Can you believe that? Unbelievable!"

Mike was amazed as well. When he had laid out their plan, he thought they would just wound the lions enough to make them go away. He had no idea that the power of their homemade bows and arrows was enough to kill a full-grown lion. Birds? Yes. Lions? No. It appeared all of the hard work in constructing their arrow tips and bows had saved their lives. However, there was one more question they needed to ask, "Are there any more lions out there?"

The boys decided it might be safer for them to spend the night in the tree rather than get back on the ground and try to make a dash to their cave. They knew they were lucky to be able to escape these two lionesses, and they did not want to press their luck any more. They each took out a small section of rope from their pack and tied it around them and the trunk of the tree. It was not the most comfortable manner of going to sleep, but it would keep them from accidentally drifting off to sleep and falling fifty feet out of the tree. Neither of them slept much that night, but when the morning came and there were still no more lions around, they decided it was time to come down.

"Look how big she is," commented Rich as he stepped from the trunk onto the body of the lion. "I'll be she must weigh three hundred pounds or more. Can you eat lion?"

"Rich, I don't know but we are darn sure going to find out! Make a fire while I get us some lion meat." No sooner had these words came out of his mouth and Mike heard a throaty cough near him. Then there was a roar and the soft sound of padded feet coming his way.

It was the lion he had shot and the arrow was still in its side. The lioness stopped short of him and just stood there looking at Mike as if he was a pork chop. She then slowly started walking toward him. Mike turned to face the lion with his spear toward the lioness. He had no time to string an arrow into his bow, so as he had seen others do, he planted the butt of the spear in the ground and held the spear with both hands.

The lion pounced when she was about ten feet from Mike. Mike held his ground and guided the spear's tip into the underbelly and ribcage of the lion. Rich could not see what happened after that because he was on the other side of the tree. All he saw was the lion leap and fall on top of Mike.

"Mike! Mike! Are you okay?" yelled Rich. "Mike!"

"Get it off! Get it off!" he heard a muffled cry from under the lioness.

Rich ran over to the lion that was now dead, grabbed a paw and pulled it off Mike. Mike had blood all over him, but the blood was not his. It was the lion's blood. The spear had finished the job that the arrow did not do. Horrified, Rich asked again, "Mike, are you okay?"

"Yea, but that darn lion must have weighed more than three hundred pounds! Golly she was heavy."

"Rich asked, "How did you learn to do that?"

Mike asked, "Do what?"

"You know, kill a lion with a spear!"

"You didn't know I was part Watusi warrior, Rich?" he laughed. "Actually, I saw it in a movie I watched at our theater back home. It was all about how these African kids had to kill a lion before they could become a man, and they used a spear to do that. I guess I'm a man now, huh?"

Rich just laughed and said, "You got my vote! Now, let's cut us some steaks and eat these things before something else tries to eat us!"

The boys took their time skinning the lions and cutting some prime steaks, which they roasted over a fire under their tree. "Doesn't taste like chicken," Rich commented.

"I think it tastes more like pork," Mike relayed. "A little bitter, but pretty darn good. I wonder what we would taste like to them?"

"Chicken," laughed Rich.

CHAPTER 14 – HOME SWEET HOME

With their packs filled with cooked lion meat and each carrying a lion skin to be made into shoes, shirts, and pants, the boys left the next morning and headed back to their cave. They ran into a puma along the way, which took one look at them and acted as if he thought they might make a nice supper for him. Once he got a whiff of their lion scent, he decided he would go find an easier target to dine on and ran off into the trees.

"I don't think I will bathe for a week or more if that's the kind of reception we are going to get with all these things that want to eat us," laughed Mike.

"Oh yes you are," pleaded Rich. "You stink to high heaven! You are going swimming in the ocean as soon as we get to the cave. Ah, home sweet home, after you have a bath."

As they knew it would, it took them the rest of the day to arrive at their cave. Since they were arriving at the "back door" of their cave, they went up their homemade ladder rather than walk clear around the large hill to the mouth of their cave. After tying the rope round their packs and the lion pelts, Rich went up first and thanks to his strength, pulled all of their gear up the ladder.

Mike went up behind Rich and made sure their packs did not hang up on the ladder. Rich went through their back entrance pulling packs and lion pelts with him. When he got to a turn, he had to push their packs and the pelts around a bend before he could push them any further.

Just as the pelts went around the corner, a gunshot rang out and a bullet went hurtling through the lion's pelts and into the wall near Rich's head. "Hey! What was that?" yelled Rich.

Both Mike and Rich could hear much muffled conversation on the other side of the packs and lion pelts, and finally Rich peeked around the corner to discover who was shooting at them. It was his mom and dad!

"Mom! Dad! It's Mike and Rich. What are you shooting at us for?"

"Oh my God," their mom said. "It's the boys! Don't' shoot honey!"

Both of the boys pushed the packs and lion pelts aside and ran to their parents who were standing there in the cave. Their dad had a smoking rifle in his hands, and their mom stood there with open arms for both of them. They decided their mom looked safer than their dad did, so they both went to her first.

"Sorry boys, I thought you were a lion coming up the small tunnel from the back of the cave. Glad I'm not such a great shot."

Rich just laughed and commented, "But Dad, you are a great shot. You hit the lion and missed your son!"

Mike asked, "How long have you been here?"

"About two days. We saw your signal fire's smoke and came directly here. We thought you might be dead, but were relieved to see the handiwork that you left here," as he pointed to all the stuff that Rich had left behind. "As soon as I saw that pile, I knew it had to be my sons, Mike and Rich. Rich wanted to take everything and Mike made him leave it," their dad laughed. "Come on guys; let's get back to the boat and home. Mike, you need a swim in the ocean. You reek!"

All four laughed and after packing up those things they thought appropriate as a remembrance to the adventure, they all headed down to the beach to the waiting skiff. Mike started to get in the small rowboat.

Dad said, "Oh, no you don't," as he caught Mike by the arm and nodded at Rich to grab his other arm.

They threw Mike into the ocean and made him stay there until all of the lion's blood and scent washed away in the beautiful clear sea. They then rowed out to their anchored ship and steamed toward home, and another future adventure.

The End of This Adventure …. The Beginning of Another